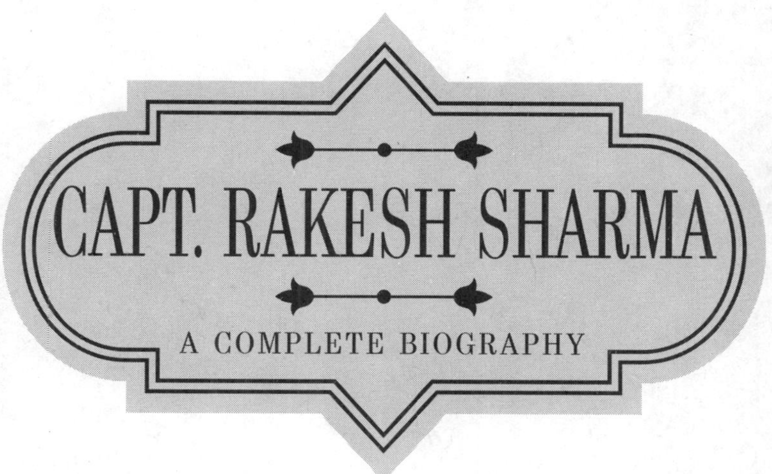
CAPT. RAKESH SHARMA
A COMPLETE BIOGRAPHY

AF531660

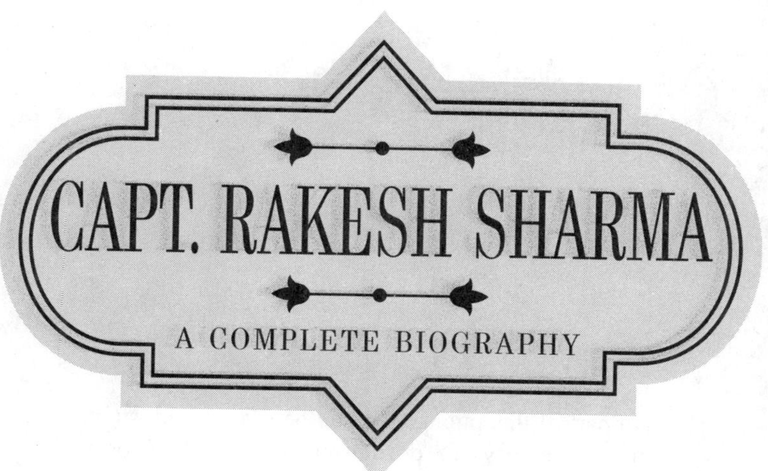

HARSHA SHARMA

Published by
PRABHAT PRAKASHAN PVT. LTD.
4/19 Asaf Ali Road,
New Delhi-110 002 (INDIA)
e-mail: prabhatbooks@gmail.com

ISBN 978-93-5488-639-3
CAPT. RAKESH SHARMA: A COMPLETE BIOGRAPHY
by Harsha Sharma

Edition
First, 2023

Price
₹ 250 (Rupees Two Hundred Fifty Only)

Printed at
Japan Art, Delhi

Introduction

Wing Commander Rakesh Sharma, a former Indian Air Force pilot, is the first Indian to go into space. Rakesh Sharma was born in Patiala on January 13, 1949. He joined the Indian Air Force in the year 1970 as a fighter pilot. During the Indo-Pak war of 1971, he flew at least 21 times. He was the first Indian and the 138th person to travel in space.

On April 3, 1984, Rakesh Sharma went into space on a Soyuz T-11 with two Soviet cosmonauts, Commander Yuri Vasilyevich Malyshev and Flight Engineer Gennady Mikhailovich Strekalov. In a joint programme of the Indian Space Research Organization (ISRO) and the Soviet Intercosmos Space Programme, the former Indian Air Force pilot spent 7 days, 21 hours and 40 minutes in space.

While in space, Rakesh Sharma carried out many experiments, including taking photographs of India from outer space and analyzing the effects of yoga during weightlessness. During the mission, he carried out many experiments in zero gravity.

"I orbited the Earth and our scientists carried out many experiments using our instruments. In that sense, the opportunity was well utilised." Rakesh Sharma said.

One of Rakesh Sharma's most memorable experiences was his conversation with the then Prime Minister Indira Gandhi, who asked what India looked like from space. Rakesh Sharma replied, "Sare Jahan Se Achcha Hindostan Hamara."

Among his most unparalleled experiences in space, sunrise and sunset were the most beautiful moments.

The mission lasted for about eight days. On April 11, 1984, Rakesh Sharma and his two-member Soviet crew returned to Earth and landed in Kazakhstan.

He is also the first Indian to receive the 'Hero of the Soviet Union' award. He also received the 'Ashok Chakra' along with his Russian co-astronauts.

Sharma joined Hindustan Aeronautics as its chief test pilot in 1987 after retiring from the Air Force. He left it in 2001 after becoming chairman of the Automated Work Flow Board.

This is the thrilling story of Rakesh Sharma's journey from pilot to an astronaut.

❑

Contents

First Indian in Space

While space travel was considered a revolutionary step in the field of science, it was nothing less than a thrilling experience for a human being. Although the story of America's and the Soviet Union's space flight was very old and many of their astronauts had successfully travelled to space, someone from a developing country who was a new player in space science getting the privilege of traveling into space was no less than a marvel. However, this miracle did happen and Indian Air Force's Squadron Leader (Wing Commander Later on) Rakesh Sharma created a new history by traveling to space. About 38 years ago, on the historic day of April 3, 1984, Rakesh Sharma, along with two other Soviet cosmonauts, went on a space journey aboard the Soyuz T-11 spacecraft. During this journey, he stayed in space for about 8 days at the Salyut-7, the space station established by Soviet Russia. During that time, he took many pictures of northern India from space and practiced yoga along with flying without gravity. Rakesh Sharma was the 138th astronaut in the world to travel to space. Rakesh Sharma's space travel is a matter of pride for every Indian.

Birth and Education

Astronaut Rakesh Sharma was born on January 13, 1949, in Patiala, Punjab. His mother's name is Tripta Sharma and his father's name is Devendra Sharma. After Rakesh's birth, his parents moved to Hyderabad, a city in Andhra Pradesh. Rakesh was admitted to St. George Grammar School. After completing his schooling, Rakesh Sharma joined Osmania University in Hyderabad for his graduation. During his graduation, he was selected to the National Defence Academy (NDA) in the year 1966 and went for training.

Career

It is said that Rakesh Sharma was fond of subjects related to science since childhood. From his school days, he had started showing interest in electronics. After completing his training in the National Defence Academy as a cadet, Rakesh Sharma's wish came true when he was recruited as a test pilot in the Indian Air Force in the year 1970. In the Indian Air Force, he soon got an opportunity to demonstrate his ability to fly fighter aircraft. During the Indo-Pakistan War of 1971, he proved his mettle by successfully piloting a MiG aircraft on the battlefield. Due to his merit, Rakesh Sharma rose to the rank of Squadron Leader in the Indian Air Force in the year 1984. Meanwhile, on September 20, 1982, Rakesh Sharma was selected along with another Indian citizen Ravish Malhotra for a joint space mission of India and the Soviet Union. Under this programme, either of the two was going to get a chance to travel to space.

Actually, under this joint mission of India's space science organization 'ISRO' and the Soviet Union's 'Intercosmos', three astronauts from both countries were to travel to space by spacecraft to carry out the study of space. Out of the three astronauts, two were to be selected from the Soviet Union and one from India. However, both the Indian nominees, Rakesh Sharma and Ravish Malhotra, were sent to the Soviet Union's space station Baikonur in Kazakhstan for pre-travel training. Rakesh Sharma aced this training and finally was selected for space travel. Then came the historic day of April 3, 1984, when Rakesh Sharma, along with two Soviet cosmonauts, flew to distant space in the Soyuz T-11 spacecraft. After take-off, the three cosmonauts successfully reached the orbital station Salyut-7, established by the Soviet Union in space.

With this historic space mission, India became the 14th country in the world to send a human being to space. Rakesh Sharma spent approximately 8 days (7 days 21 hours and 40 minutes) in space. During this time, this space team conducted 33 experiments relating to scientific and technical studies. Rakesh Sharma was given the responsibility of conducting studies especially relating to bio-medicine and remote sensing.

During the space mission, the joint team together with the officials of the Soviet Union from Moscow also held a joint conversation with Indira Gandhi, the then Prime Minister of the country in New Delhi. During this conversation, Indira Gandhi asked Rakesh Sharma an interesting question- "How does India look from space?"

Rakesh Sharma also gave an equally interesting answer to Mrs. Gandhi's interesting question – "Sare

Jahan Se Achcha Hindostan Hamara". At that time, this conversation between Indira Gandhi and Rakesh Sharma became a topic of discussion in the newspapers around the country although it was also reported at the time that some religious fundamentalist groups had expressed their displeasure over Rakesh Sharma's space journey. Supporting their stand, those groups said that going to the holy planets was against religion. But the Indian public struggling for progress in the field of science thought it better to celebrate the achievement of Rakesh Sharma and rejected the views of those fundamentalists and ignored their voiced.

Achievements

Upon returning from his space travel, Rakesh Sharma received a warm welcome in India.

The Government of India honoured him with 'Ashok Chakra', the highest award given for bravery during peacetime.

As an expression of its deep friendship with India, the Soviet Union also honoured Rakesh Sharma with the 'Hero of Soviet Union' award.

In the year 1987, Rakesh Sharma retired from Indian Air Force as a Wing Commander. After retirement, he briefly served as a test pilot in Hindustan Aeronautics Limited.

In 2001, he left Hindustan Aeronautics and became the chairman of a company called 'Automated Workflow'.

Later, in the year 2006, Rakesh Sharma was nominated to the board of the 'Indian Space Research Organisation'.

❑

Achievements in Space

Rakesh Sharma is a simple and gentle person. He is married to Madhu Sharma, who is Colonel P. N. Sharma's daughter. Both husband and wife are also fluent in Russian. His son is named Kapil and his daughter is named Kritika. Both of them are associated with the field of film/media.

Life Events

Year	Events
1949	Born on January 13th in a Gaur Brahmin family in Patiala, Punjab.

1966	Selection for National Defence Academy.
1970	Appointment to the position of Test Pilot in the Indian Air Force.
1971	Had the honour of flying the Mikoyan a fighter aircraft manufactured in Russia.
1982	Rakesh Sharma was selected for the India-Russia joint space mission. Under this mission, he would have the honour of undertaking space travel.
1984	On 3rd April, Rakesh Sharma flew into space with two Russian astronauts. He became the first Indian to get this honour.
1987	Retired from Indian Air Force as Wing Commander.
1987	Rendered his services to 'Hindustan Aeronautics Limited' as a test pilot.
2006	Nominated as a member of the board of the Indian Space Research Organisation.

Selection for Space Travel

Every child across the country knows the name of Wing Commander Rakesh Sharma. He became the first Indian to orbit space in Russia's Soyuz T-11 spacecraft in April 1984. He spent 7 days, 21 hours, and 40 minutes in space with two Soviet cosmonauts, Yuri Vasilyevich Malyshev and flight engineer Gennady Mikhailovich Strekalov.

Born on January 13, 1949, in Patiala, Rakesh Sharma served as an Air Force pilot in the Indian Armed Forces before becoming an astronaut.

In January 1982, when it was decided that an Indian would travel to space on a Soviet spacecraft, Squadron Leader Rakesh Sharma volunteered for this very challenging mission. After a very difficult selection process, which also included the most accurate medical test, he was selected as one of two astronaut candidates from among 150 qualified and experienced pilots of the Indian Air Force.

❑

Selection and Training

India's first astronaut Rakesh Sharma's name is written in golden letters in history. Rakesh Sharma, who became a Wing Commander in the Indian Air Force, is considered a hero in many countries along with India. A strong-willed and ambitious Rakesh Sharma used to fix faulty electrical equipment in his early days.

Inclination towards Technology

Rakesh Sharma was an intelligent student. He used to fix electronic devices without any training even during his adolescence years. His inclination towards technology took him on the journey of being India's first astronaut. He did his schooling at Nizam's College, Osmania University, Hyderabad, and joined the National Defence Academy in 1966. In 1970, he joined the Indian Air Force.

Taking the wind out of Pakistan's sails

Squadron Leader Rakesh Sharma took part in the 1971 war against Pakistan. In this battle, Rakesh Sharma took the wind out of the enemy's sails from his MiG aircraft. His skill and courage in the war were appreciated and he was talked about across the country. Indira Gandhi, the Prime Minister of that time, praised Rakesh Sharma for his courage and wisdom and called him a true soldier of the country.

More Than Seven Days in Space

In 1982, Rakesh Sharma was selected from India for the joint space mission Cosmos between India and the Soviet Union. Rakesh Sharma was sent along with other astronauts on Soyuz T-11 for the space mission in 1984. Rakesh Sharma became the first person from India to go to space.

Hero

Rakesh Sharma took photographs of some parts of northern India from space and also received training to survive without gravity. When Rakesh Sharma reached space, the then Prime Minister of India Indira Gandhi was connected with him. Indira Gandhi asked, "What does India look like from space?" In response to this, Rakesh Sharma said, "I can say without any hesitation that 'Saare Jahan Se Achcha Hindostan Hamara'." The video clip of Rakesh's reply is present on social media. With this reply, Rakesh Sharma made a special place in the hearts of people.

This is a couplet by Muhammad Iqbal, which Rakesh used to sing after the national anthem every day during his school days.

Rakesh Sharma says, "I remember it very well. There was nothing like patriotic hysteria in it. India looked really beautiful from space."

At that time, the 'New York Times' wrote that India would not have its own human space travel for a long time and that for a very long time, Rakesh Sharma would remain the only Indian to go to space.

Declared Hero by the Soviet Union

When Rakesh Sharma returned after completing the space mission, he was awarded 'Ashok Chakra' by the

Government of India. The Soviet Union honoured him with the title of 'Hero of the Soviet Union'. Apart from this, Rakesh Sharma was honoured with many other awards. Rakesh Sharma retired from the Indian Air Force as a Wing Commander and was appointed as the Chief pilot of 'Hindustan Aeronautics Limited', a Navratna company that manufactures aircraft.

The Soviet Union had proposed to Indira Gandhi to include two Indians in the mission. She had no option other than Air Force officers. At that time, 'ISRO' also lacked resources. In such a situation, two officers from the 'Indian Air Force', Rakesh Sharma and Ravish Malhotra were given 18 months of rigorous training.

Rigorous Training

Astronaut training describes the complex process of preparing astronauts for their space missions around the world before, during and after the flight, which includes medical tests, physical training, extravehicular Activity (EVA) training, training procedures, rehabilitation process as well as training for the experiments that they would carry out while in space.

In this, virtual and physical training facilities are integrated to familiarize the astronauts with the conditions that they would face during all phases of flight and prepare the astronauts for the microgravity environment.

The selection and training of astronauts are integrated processes to ensure that crew members are qualified for space missions. To train astronauts on general and specific aspects, the training has been classified into the following categories-

Basic Training

During basic training, the trainees are trained in medicine, languages, robotics and piloting, space systems engineering, space systems organization and aerospace engineering.

Advanced Training

During advanced training, astronauts learn about the operation of specific systems and the skills associated with their assigned positions in a space mission. This specific training for astronauts typically requires 18 months to complete. It is important to ensure the physical and mental health of astronauts before, during and after the mission. The expertise includes subjects such as additional activity, robotics, language, diving and flight training.

Launching and Landing

Launching and landing have various effects on astronauts, with the most notable effects being motion sickness and orthostatic and cardiovascular side effects from motion in space. Space motion sickness is a phenomenon that can occur within minutes of changing gravity. Symptoms range from drowsiness and headache to nausea and vomiting. About three-quarters of the astronauts experience space motion sickness, the effects of which rarely last more than two days. There is a risk of motion sickness after the flight, although this happens only after space missions of long duration.

Operating in Orbit

Astronauts are trained to prepare for conditions during launch as well as the harsh environment in space. The purpose of this training is to prepare the crew for events that fall under two broad categories—events related to the operation of spacecraft (internal events) and events related to the space environment (external events).

During training, astronauts become familiar with the engineering systems of spacecraft, including spacecraft propulsion, its thermal control, and life support systems. In addition, astronauts receive training in orbital mechanics, scientific experimentation, observation of the earth, and astronomy. This training is especially important for the mission as an astronaut has to handle multiple systems. Astronauts are trained to prepare for events that may threaten their health, the health of the crew, or the successful completion of the mission.

The following types of events can occur—failure of an important life support system, capsule depression, fire, and other life-threatening events. In addition to requiring training for hazardous events, astronauts also need to be trained to ensure the successful completion of their mission.

External Events

External events more broadly refer to the ability to live and work in the extreme environment of space. That includes adaptation to microgravity (or weightlessness), isolation, confinement and radiation. Difficulties associated with living and working in microgravity include spatial disorientation, motion sickness, and vertigo. During missions of long-duration, astronauts often experience isolation and imprisonment. This is known to limit the performance of the astronaut crew and hence the aim of the training is to prepare the astronauts for such challenges.

Scientific Experiments

Scientific experimentation has historically been an important element of human spaceflight. Learning how to successfully perform these experiments is an important part of astronaut training because it optimizes the scientific aspect of the mission. It is important that astronauts are familiar with their assigned experiments so that they can be completed in a timely manner, with as little interference from the earth as possible.

Each astronaut is required to become proficient in one hundred or more experiments. During training, the scientists responsible for the experiments do not have direct contact with the astronauts who will carry them out. So, the scientists give instructions to the instructors, who in turn prepare the astronauts to perform the experiments.

Virtual Reality Training

Virtual Reality Training for Astronauts aims to give a comprehensive training experience to the candidates. Virtual reality has been explored as a technique for artificially exposing astronauts to the conditions and processes of space before they go into space. When the target serves as a practice tool, virtual reality is usually explored in conjunction with robotics and additional hardware to enhance the effect of immersion or trainee engagement.

Duration of Training

It takes two years of training to become a qualified astronaut. Initially, one has to undergo basic training to learn both technical and soft skills. It includes various technical courses - Life Support Systems, Orbital Mechanics, Payload Deployment, Earth Observation, Space Physiology and Medicine etc.

Appreciation by Space Experts

After his selection, Rakesh trained as a cosmonaut at the Yuri Gagarin Centre in Russia, where he proved himself with his utmost devotion and dedication and also won praise from Soviet space experts.

Squadron Leader Rakesh Sharma became the first Indian to orbit space on 3rd April 1984. He successfully completed all scientific experiments and in-space tasks assigned to him which were a part of the joint Indo-Soviet space mission.

Rakesh Sharma had taken Indian food into space with the help of the Defence Food Research Lab in Mysore.

He had packed sooji halwa, aloo chole and veg pulao, which he also shared with his fellow astronauts.

He took pictures of India from space and saved India two years of aerial photography to map the same area.

Sharma had taken photographs of the then Prime Minister Indira Gandhi, President Zail Singh, Defence Minister Venkataraman and the soil and picture of Rajghat, Mahatma Gandhi's Samadhi.

Apart from being the first Indian to go to space, Rakesh Sharma is also the first Indian to be honoured with the 'Hero of the Soviet Union' award. He was also awarded the Ashoka Chakra along with his Russian co-astronauts Yuri Malyshev and Gennady Strekalov.

The Government of India honoured him with 'Ashok Chakra', the highest gallantry peacetime award.

Sharma retired from the Indian Air Force as Wing Commander.

In the words of Rakesh Sharma-

"I cannot forget the excitement and exhilaration with what happened at that time. The training was over and we were in the capsule (spacecraft) with our checklists and imagining what would happen to us next. I was looking forward to the out-of-this-world experience I had been trained for.

As we were trained, the speed was very high as soon as the vehicle was launched and we sank into our seats. The force of gravity kept building up and we suddenly went from three and a half to three and then to zero gravity and all this happened in just 500 seconds.

It was very dramatic in itself and then we saw the Earth from space - it was a spectacular sight. Everyone first searched for their country. Then we saw India, which looked very beautiful because our country has different characteristics—a long coastline, plains, forests, deserts, our colours and texture and finally the Himalayas.

Those eight days in space were extremely enjoyable. It is hard to imagine the immense beauty that was there. It was all a cosmic coincidence. I have never seen such a beautiful coincidence. That was very pleasant, because we, our homes, the planet are nothing but a small part of that universe.

After returning from space, my whole life changed. Wherever I went, I was recognized. Although a lot of time has passed now, people have a short memory and I don't look the same anymore I no longer need to hide from people like I had to.

Why was the interest in space exploration aroused again? Regarding this, I think that such is the nature of man that he keeps on searching for something new. Civilizations started in Africa and spread all across. Then we made communication devices. We then built ships and went out and explored other places and soon we spread around. Now, that we have come to know the whole earth, it is natural that we start looking towards the new world.

We are making good use of the resources available on the earth. But they can end anytime. That is why we are compelled to look towards other planets. Also, there is no backup of the human genome (a set of genes) in case a cataclysmic event occurs. An entire civilization can be wiped out by the collision of a single satellite.

So, this is the reason why space exploration is being carried out. Before that, a race was going on between the then Soviets and the Americans. They proved to the world that both countries are capable of going to the moon and bringing the soil from there. They couldn't do more than that because the technology at that time was limited and that's why no one went back.

But now that we are technologically advanced and we have reasons for it, new opportunities are also opening up.

The private sector is also taking interest in this although it is starting with tourism which is just another business. I think we are at the crossroads of very exciting times."

❑

Meeting God in Space!

After Rakesh Sharma, the first Indian to go to space, returned from space, people in India would often ask whether he had met God in space.

To this, he would reply, "No, I did not find God there."

Rakesh Sharma was always surrounded by fans for a year after his return from space. He would always be visiting some places and stay in hotels and guest houses.

He says, “Many women who met me introduced me to their children saying, “This uncle had gone to the moon.”

Elderly women used to offer blessings. Fans would even tear his clothes. They would scream for his autograph. The political leaders would take him to rallies in their areas to garner votes.

Recalling the old days, he says, “It was a completely different feeling. I was exhausted and tired of this crazy fanfare. I had to keep laughing all the time.”

Rakesh Sharma joined the Indian Air Force at the age of 21 and used to fly supersonic jet fighter aircraft.

He flew 21 times in the 1971 war with Pakistan. He was not even 23 years old at that time.

At the age of 25, he was the best pilot in the Air Force. He had walked 35 times in space and he was the 138th person to do so in space.

Rakesh Sharma was selected from among the 50 fighter pilots who underwent the test. Apart from him, Ravish Malhotra was also selected through this test and both of them were sent to Russia for training.

A year before going into space, Rakesh Sharma and Ravish Malhotra had gone to Star City, which is 70 km from Moscow and a training centre for astronauts.

Rakesh recalls, "It was very cold there. We had to walk from one building to another in snow."

He was faced with the challenge of learning the Russian language as quickly as possible because most of his training was going to be conducted in the Russian language. Every day he used to learn Russian for six to seven hours. As a result, he learned Russian acceptably well in three months.

His food was also taken care of. Olympic trainers monitored his stamina, speed and strength and trained him.

During the training itself, he was told that he had been selected and that Ravish Malhotra would be his backup.

Rakesh Sharma humbly admits, "It was not so difficult."

On April 3, 1984, Rakesh Sharma and two Russian cosmonauts, Yuri Malyshev and Gennady Strekalov, left for space in a Soviet rocket. The flight took off from a space station in the then Soviet Republic of Kazakhstan.

Rakesh Sharma recalls that moment, "It was very boring when we were leaving because we had practiced it so much that it was like a routine."

Was he also anxious while going from Earth to space?

Rakesh replied, "Look, I was the 138th person to go into space. 137 people had come back alive. So, there was no reason to panic."

Yoga In Space

Rakesh Sharma was the first person to practice yoga in space. By practicing yoga, he tried to find out whether it can help reduce the effect of gravity.

He said, "It was very difficult. You don't feel any weight under your feet. You keep floating in the air. That's why we had to come up with a way to steady ourselves."

Never-ending Trials

At that time, Indians were very curious as to who among Sharma and Malhotra would have the honour of being the first Indian astronaut. In the end, Rakesh Sharma won the bet. Thus, on September 20, 1982, Rakesh Sharma's name was finalized through the Indian Space Research Organization (ISRO) for the Intercosmos Mission. Ravish Malhotra was ready to replace Rakesh Sharma in any adverse situation, but it was not required.

Rakesh Sharma achieved this position after passing through rigorous tests. There was also a criterion wherein he had to stay alone in a closed room for three days. His test did not end here. After being selected for the mission, while he was engaged in intensive exercises at Russia's Yuri Gagarin Space Centre for mission tests, his six-year-old daughter Manasi passed away in India. He did not get distracted by the incident and kept himself focused on his goal. The hopes of the whole country were pinned on him and he did not let those hopes go in vain.

His experimentation in space was greatly boosted and during his stay in space, he conducted a total of 33 experiments. These included experiments designed to counteract the effects of weightlessness.

His achievements made many Indian youths interested in the field of space. Over time, names of some Indian-origin astronauts, from Kalpana Chawla to Sunita Williams, emerged, who became part of the missions of the US space agency NASA.

❑

The Tough Road to Space

Today India has its own powerful rockets to reach the Moon and Mars. Additionally, today, the Indian Space Research Organization is carrying out huge commercial missions. ISRO also set a world record in 2017 by launching 104 satellites simultaneously through PSLV. At the same time, India's Chandrayaan-1 and Mangalyaan missions have attracted attention of the whole world.

Although some people do not mention Rakesh Sharma's contribution to the development of the Indian

Space Research Organization it is true that it is because of Rakesh Sharma that we are talking about sending humans to space today. Rakesh Sharma had to go through many difficult tests before becoming an astronaut. He also had to undergo several tests at the Institute of Aerospace Medicine, Bangalore. Once he was locked in a room for 72 hours. He was then given rigorous training for nearly two years at the Yuri Gagarin Cosmonaut Training Centre in Star City, Moscow.

Along with Rakesh Sharma, Ravish Malhotra was also selected for the final training. Both were pilots in the Indian Air Force. This was done because an astronaut has to be on stand-by. In the end, Rakesh Sharma was selected as the astronaut.

It is true that India had got this opportunity because of her friendship with Russia, but it is also true that this achievement inspired us to become completely self-reliant in the field of space. We developed indigenous resources rapidly and achieved many important milestones in the area. Today, we have powerful rockets to take us to the Moon and Mars. Today, we are not only bringing our important satellites into Earth's orbit through our own rockets but we are also passing the benefits of our technology to other countries.

Living in a state of weightlessness in space is very challenging. It has an adverse effect on the body. But Rakesh Sharma had made special preparations to deal with weightlessness. He practised yoga for ten minutes every day. He practised yoga even in the conditions of zero gravity. By practising yoga, he demonstrated that India's traditional wisdom can also prove useful in dealing with difficult situations like weightlessness.

For a long time, we have been trying to find signs of extra-terrestrial life on Mars. The presence of extra-terrestrial life is an eternal question, the answer to which is sought by everyone.

Space is one such area where we cannot depend on the capability of just one or two countries. In this context, India's Chandrayaan-1 mission should be remembered, which showed the world for the first time that there is water on the moon. This means that India can make a big contribution to unveiling the mysteries of space. Rakesh Sharma, the first Indian astronaut, has demonstrated that we have ample opportunities to move forward in space.

Rakesh spent a long time in Bangalore. Now he lives in the beautiful 'hill town' of Coonoor in Tamil Nadu. After retiring, Rakesh Sharma built his dream house here in Coonoor. The roofs of this house are slanted, the bathrooms are equipped with solar heaters and the rain water gets collected at one place.

He is also the non-executive chairman of Cadila Labs, a Bangalore-based company. The company provides intelligence automation, especially to companies in the insurance sector.

❑

Any One!

Rakesh Sharma or Ravish Malhotra? Both were shortlisted. Both were selected. Both were trained. How did Ravish feel upon seeing fellow Air Force officer Rakesh Sharma, the first Indian going into space?

Ravish Malhotra and Rakesh Sharma were more than just fellow citizens whom fate had secretly brought together. Both of them were of Punjabi origin. Both were adherents of the strict military code to which wingmen are bound although at the last hour only one of them was to be given a return ticket to the universe.

On April 3, 1984, Soyuz T-11 took off from Baikonur Cosmodrome at exactly 13:08 Coordinated Universal Time (UTC). The launch facility, hidden in the backwoods of the USSR, was located in modern-day Kazakhstan—away from the prying eyes of the Americans, with whom the Soviets were walking lockstep in the space race. After boarding the spacecraft, Rakesh Sharma saw that the earth was shrinking into a tiny particle on the horizon. As the Soyuz T-11 entered outer space, the engine noise was gradually replaced by the silence of the steppe.

Ravish Malhotra saw his companion going skyward from the control centre of the Baikonur Cosmodrome. Ravish said in an interview, "We knew from the beginning that only one of us would go to space with the Russians and the other would be on standby." Malhotra, 79, says that the spartan lifestyle he led in Moscow so many years ago kept him in good shape.

He says, "I still do basic exercises for about 45 minutes a day. Apart from this, I walk about 35 km every week."

Ravish Malhotra was born on Christmas in 1943—the year of the Bengal famine. The British were waging wars on several fronts as they struggled to maintain their hold on their colonial empire. Malhotra, who lived in Lahore, was largely protected from the political turmoil around him. But things changed after India's tryst with destiny. On midnight of August 15, 1947, when the world was sleeping, India woke up to independence. The spectre of partition passed on the map of the subcontinent. Millions were displaced. Thousands lost their lives.

Malhotra says, "I was only five years old when my family moved from Lahore to Delhi. I was very young and I don't remember any details except that we stayed with my uncle in Delhi after fleeing from Lahore."

Eventually, his parents finally settled in Calcutta, switching grounds again with Ravish and his three siblings. The Malhotra brothers studied at St. Thomas School, Calcutta, which is one of the oldest institutions in the country. After graduation, young Ravish appeared for the entrance exam of the prestigious National Defence Academy (NDA). He succeeded.

"Three of my cousins were in the Navy and I had made up my mind to join them," he says. However, fate intervened and instead of his first preference, he was inducted into the Indian Air Force. Malhotra became a commissioned officer in 1963 and was inducted into the 'Vampire Squadron', a group of pilots who had flown the British fighter jets of the same name. He was posted at the Air Force base in Barrackpore, a suburb of Calcutta, not far from his childhood home. Malhotra says, "It was a stroke of destiny that I did not join the Navy but the Air Force. I am glad it happened, otherwise I would not have been a part of the great adventure that was to come."

Malhotra flew the Vampire jet as a shrewd pilot. But soon he surpassed the aircrafts of World War II era. As he explains, "The more effort you put in, you upgrade to a better pilot."

Malhotra was later shifted to airports at forward posts like Ambala and Pathankot. He also had the opportunity to fly more sophisticated aircrafts such as the Dassault Mystere, American F-111 bomber and indigenous HAL HF-24 Marut.

When asked about the factors that determine the fleet composition of the Indian Air Force, he says, "As far as I know, the Defence Procurement Procedures have been laid down by the Ministry of Defence and they are revised from time to time to suit the requirements of the IAF. The procedures will be similar."

Eventually, Malhotra graduated to the cockpit of the Soviet-built Sukhoi Su-22, the then fighter jet of the Indian Air Force. Meanwhile, trouble was brewing on the Western Front, which required Malhotra to return to his homeland.

The Wounds of War

In 1971, Pakistan conducted preventive airstrikes on 11 airports in India, prompting New Delhi to enter the war in East Pakistan. The Indian Air Force was deployed and it carried out air strikes to support the advance of the ground troops in a two-front war. Malhotra was stationed at a base in North India and was part of a fighter squadron tasked with launching cross-border strikes.

He says, "I flew a Sukhoi-22, a ground attack aircraft, and made 17 sorties across the border in support of our forces on the Western Front. Several times, I returned with bullet holes in my plane from enemy anti-aircraft guns. By the grace of God, I was very fortunate unlike some of my colleagues, whom we tragically lost." Some members of his squadron were taken as prisoners of war and some were eventually deported back to India.

Malhotra says, "Wing Commander Dilip Parulkar and I were part of the same squadron. His plane was shot down over Pakistan and he was taken prisoner. He escaped from the prison, but he was captured again. Eventually, he was returned to India. We are in touch." Parulkar's capture and eventual homecoming is the subject of the crowdfunded film 'The Great Indian Escape'. Others weren't so lucky. Some went missing and they were not heard of. They were presumed dead.

The war ended with a decisive victory for India. East Pakistan became independent and Bangladesh was born. Life returned to normal and restive peace prevailed. After the war, Malhotra was selected to take a test pilot course at the USAF Test Pilot School at Edwards Air Force Base in California. He says, "Being a test pilot, selection for astronaut training was a plus point." He was then shortlisted to participate in the Indo-Soviet space mission. "I considered it a great honour. Can you imagine that one of the two people selected for the mission would be only one out of our population of over a billion Indians?"

The selection criteria included excellent fitness of mind and body. There was a prerequisite for one to be considered as a pilot, as Malhotra elaborated, "Experience as a criterion was another plus point as it included a better understanding of avionic systems."

From a large batch of candidates, four were eventually shortlisted for extensive trials at the Institute of Aerospace Medicine in Bangalore and sent to Moscow for further medical evaluation. At the end of the final medical trials in Moscow, Rakesh Sharma and Ravish Malhotra were selected.

It was followed by rigorous training for the better part of two years at the Yuri Gagarin Cosmonaut Training Centre in Star City. The medium of instruction was Russian. Malhotra recalls, "It took us about three months to master the language. This was a mandatory requirement as all the dials and instruments of the spacecraft had inscriptions in Russian. Also, the Soviet cosmonauts and team members did not speak English." Language lessons were followed by classroom theory sessions on space flight.

Star City cadets had to adapt themselves to various systems on the Soyuz T-11, including a life support system. They also had to practice emergency procedures that would have to be followed while flying the spacecraft. Their daily routine included theory classes in the morning followed by practical training on the spacecraft simulator as well as mock-ups of the space station in the afternoon. The crew of astronauts would go to the gym in the evening to improve their fitness level.

Apart from working on the simulator, they were also trained in supernormal conditions. Malhotra says, "We were trained for the micro-gravity conditions by adapting an IL-76 aircraft to the space environment, which was fully padded on the inside. The aircraft performed an 'over the top' manoeuvre, which is similar to the outer loop. This makes the position of gravity close to zero for about 45 to 50 seconds." During this period, the astronauts are trained to manoeuvre in zero gravity conditions in space. Several such manoeuvres were performed on each test flight and many such flights were carried out.

Malhotra says, "We had to get acquainted with some special equipment, such as space suits to be used during launch and descent. We were also specially trained in the sea." Although the astronauts' families were allowed to join them during the training period in Moscow, they were allowed to dine in the mess hall. Dietary intake was controlled and physical exercise was monitored.

Malhotra says, "This was done to ensure peak levels of fitness and reduce the chances of falling ill during space flight. All the astronauts followed a strict fitness regime, although they were allowed to attend programmes." Malhotra says, "The food was basically Russian cuisine as we had to eat in a special mess facility. As far as drinks were concerned, I enjoyed the odd beer during the weekend. The Russians loved vodka."

The nature of their training meant that they were restricted from interacting with anyone during the work week. Over the weekend, they could interact with Indian embassy officials and diplomats, especially the defence attaches stationed in Moscow. Malhotra says, “It was natural for us to get used to the Russian culture. In defence services, we travel a lot and so dealing with the new environment was not difficult for our families.” The training, despite the competitive nature of the programme, brought about a kinship between the participants. Some friendships last a lifetime.

Ricky and Mallu

Sharma and Malhotra knew each other before their trip to the Soviet Union. “We were collaborators at the Aircraft and Systems Testing Establishment in Bangalore,” says Malhotra. However, the two became close friends during their stay in the USSR. They were allies, whose fates were intertwined with each other.

Rakesh became Ricky and Ravish became Mallu. Malhotra says, “Everyone used to call him Ricky. Malhotras are called Mallus in the Air Force. They were tasked with conducting specific tests in zero gravity, one of which was to study the effects of yoga in space. Malhotra no longer practices yoga, but some other thoughts were running through his mind during the tough training programme in Star City. The Soviet Union was infamous for its lack of transparency. External inspection of their facilities was not allowed, but Malhotra was unconcerned.

Malhotra explains, "I never felt concerned about the safety of Russian equipment. They had very strong systems and were very advanced in the field of metallurgy. In fact, Russian spacecraft operate at 760 mm of pressure, which is the same as on Earth. When compared, NASA's spacecraft operates on 480 mm of pure oxygen." Soyuz T-11 took off from Baikonur on April 3, 1984. There was no technical glitch. Rakesh Sharma and two other astronauts— Yuri Malyshev and Gennady Strekalov were launched into orbit.

Moving on with the Mission

Malhotra says, "I was disappointed, but you accept it and move on with the mission." He says that the final decision on who will go to space was taken by the Defense Ministry in New Delhi. More than three decades later, Malhotra insists that there was never any rivalry between the two. He says, "Rakesh and I are very good friends and have mutual respect and admiration for each other. Although he lives in Coonoor we always meet whenever he is in Bangalore where I live."

Malhotra, who is 79, is still excited about advances in space technology. When asked about the Indian government's plan to send another man into space, he expressed confidence in the proposed mission, but jokingly dropped himself out of the race. He said, "Alright, this time it will be on an Indian spacecraft, which will be launched by an Indian rocket. I am sure ISRO is confident about sending our own astronauts to space. It will be a big leap for India."

Malhotra, a product of that era, is staunchly apolitical. But he sees great potential in aerospace technology as a tool of modern diplomacy. He says, "Space can be used as a foreign policy tool. A classic example of this is the launch of the South Asia satellite, which will aid the study of communications and meteorology in neighbouring countries."

He says, "As I understand, there are currently no guidelines set (for civilian astronauts). A daily exercise routine will be necessary to stay healthy before embarking on any space flight. The fitness criteria of commercial astronauts, I think, will not be as stringent as those of military astronauts."

Elon Musk-owned SpaceX recently announced that it will carry astronauts in early 2023. Japanese fashion tycoon Yusaku Maezawa will have the honour of being the first citizen on the moon. He has bought a berth on the spacecraft. But Malhotra, who has made peace with the events of 1984, is more excited about Gaganyaan—India's first crewed orbital spacecraft.

❑

Ravish Malhotra

Malhotra was born on 25th December 1943 in Lahore in formerly British India, along with three other siblings. His mother was Raj Malhotra and his father was S. C. Malhotra. His family moved from Lahore to Delhi after India gained independence from Britain and its subsequent partition in 1947.

The family stayed at Malhotra's uncle's house in Delhi before settling down in Calcutta. Malhotra studied at St. Thomas School in Calcutta. After graduation, he went to the National Defense Academy (NDA). During the selection, he was told that his vision was not good enough for the Navy and he was selected for the Air Force, which at that time was short of cadets.

After graduating from the NDA, in 1963, Malhotra was commissioned as an officer in the Indian Air Force's Vampire Squadron that flew the de Havilland Vampire. During this period, he was posted to the Indian Air Force base at Barrackpore near Calcutta. He progressively graduated to flying other aircrafts, including the F-111 bomber, Dassault Mystere, HAL HF-24 Marut, and later the Soviet Sukhoi Su-22.

Malhotra was part of the Indian Air Force fighter squadron that was tasked with carrying out air strikes on Pakistan in 1971 when that country launched attacks on India prior to the Bangladesh (East Pakistan) Liberation War. He made over 17 sorties over Pakistani airspace on a Sukhoi Su-22, where some of his allies were captured and taken prisoners of war. In a particular attack in the Pak-Jaurian sector in then-West Pakistan, heavy anti-aircraft gunfire was fired at his plane, but he managed to return to the airport in India. The war ended with the successful liberation of Bangladesh.

After the 1971 war, Malhotra was selected for the US Airforce Test Pilot School at Edwards Air Force

Base in California and later the Indo-Soviet Space Programme, a joint programme between India and the former USSR.

Malhotra became Rakesh Sharma's backup for this mission, while Sharma became the first Indian to go to space. The decision to send Sharma into space and keep Malhotra on the ground was taken in the middle of the training programme by the Defence Ministry of India. Later speaking about the decision, Malhotra said, "I was disappointed, but you accept it and go ahead with the mission." He had a good relationship with Sharma even after the mission.

After his return from the Soviet Union, Malhotra was awarded the 'Kirti Chakra' and the 'Soviet Order of Friendship of Peoples' in 1984.

On his return to India, he returned to his combat role in the Air Force and was posted as the Commanding Officer at the Hindon Air Force Station near Delhi. He took retirement from the Air Force in 1995. After his retirement from the Indian Air Force, Malhotra entered the private sector and founded Dynamic Aerospace, an aerospace manufacturing firm. The NSE-listed company manufactures aeronautical parts for customers such as

Boeing, Airbus and Bell Helicopter. He retired from the company at the age of 75. Malhotra is married to Meera Malhotra. The couple has two children and lives in Bangalore.

❑

Yuri Vasilyevich Malyshev

Yuri Vasilyevich Malyshev, a two-time Hero of the Soviet Union, undertook his first flight into space when he was 29 years old. After that, he received the title of Hero, was awarded the rank of colonel, and became a first-class astronaut.

Yuri was born on August 27, 1941, in Nikolaevsk of the Volgograd region. His family was far away from the thought that a future astronaut was growing up in their family. Yuri's parents had very worldly professions—

his father was an electrician and his mother was a kindergarten teacher.

Although Malyshev started dreaming of airplanes as a teenager he had not yet thought of space at that time as such an experience had not yet been known in the whole world.

After completing his schooling, Yuri went to the famous flying school Kachinsk to get pilot's training. He completed his studies with enthusiasm and interest and then transferred to Kharkov School, where he also trained pilots.

Yuri worked as a pilot until 1967. Then he was enrolled as a student-astronaut at the Cosmonaut Training Centre, a commanding scientific and practical base for the training of highly qualified personnel in the USSR. For two years, he underwent theoretical training; his physical abilities were also tested.

In 1976, Malyshev became a backup for the Soyuz-22 commander as per the test pilots' programme. In 1980, for the first time, Yuri Malyshev flew into space and was the commander of the Soyuz T-2 spacecraft. Aksenov Vladimir Viktorovich was his partner. Both stayed in space for about four days.

In 1984, Yuri Vasilyevich took his second flight on the Soyuz T-11 spacecraft and remained in space for more than a week. On this flight, he was accompanied by flight engineers Gennady Mikhailovich Strekalov and Rakesh Sharma. After these flights, his training as an astronaut continued. He died suddenly on November 8, 1999, at the young age of 58.

❑

Gennady Mikhailovich Strekalov

Gennady Mikhailovich Strekalov was an engineer, cosmonaut, and administrator. He flew into space five times and spent more than 268 days in space. He was twice decorated as the Hero of the Soviet Union and received the Ashok Chakra from India.

Strekalov was born on October 26, 1940, in Mytishchi, near Moscow. After graduating from NE, Strekalov did a diploma in engineering from the Bauman Moscow Higher Technical School in the year 1965.

In January 1974, he began training as a crew member for the Soyuz space mission as a flight engineer and became part of the backup crew for the Soyuz 22 mission in 1976. From October 1978, he trained as a flight engineer for the Salyut-series space stations for Soyuz missions.

His first space flight as a research engineer on Soyuz T-3's mission to the Salyut 6 station was from November 27 to December 10, 1980.

His next flight was to be to the new Salyut-7 space station. He and Vladimir Titov were the backup crew for the Soyuz T-5 mission, the first flight to the new station. The pair, along with Alexander Serebrov, launched the Soyuz T-8 in April 1983. As the spacecraft separated from the aerodynamic fairing that shielded it during launch, part of its radar system was damaged. The crew attempted a manual docking on their spacecraft using only optical instruments and guided by ground radar. But the attempt was unsuccessful and Titov had to put on brakes and dive to avoid a collision. After another attempt and using up too much of their propellant, the crew was forced to return to Earth on April 22, 1983.

Strekalov and Titov were scheduled to fly again for Salyut-7 on 26th September 1983. The mission's Soyuz-U launcher experienced a serious fuel leak minutes before launch, forcing launch control to attempt to fire the launch escape system to keep the spacecraft away.

Strekalov's next space flight with Yuri Malyshev and Indian cosmonaut Rakesh Sharma was on Soyuz T-11. The flight commenced on 3rd April 1984 from Site 31 at Baikonur and unlike Strekalov's two previous attempts, it successfully docked with the Salyut-7. The crew remained on Salyut-7 until April 11, 1984, and returned to Earth though not in the spacecraft they had gone in, but in the Soyuz T-10's re-entry module, which was already docked in space.

Strekalov subsequently took formal retirement and became the head of the civilian section of the cosmonaut department.

However, for the Russian Mir space station programme, on March 14, 1995, he flew to the Mir space station from a Soyuz TM-21. He was accompanied by Vladimir Dzhurov and American cosmonaut Norman Thagard. The mission, designated EO-18, was the first non-US launch to take an American into space. It was successful. Strekalov's schedule at Mir was hectic—the crew conducted several spacewalks to repair the station.

On July 7, 1995, the Soyuz TM-21 crew returned to Earth—though not on Soyuz but aboard the US Space Shuttle Atlantis (STS-71). Altogether the mission lasted 115 days.

Strekalov continued to work until his death. He died of cancer on December 25, 2004, at the age of 64.

❑

Rakesh Sharma: Interview

The moon and the stars have fascinated every human being, but out of billions of Indians, only one has gone close to them. Rakesh Sharma, the first Indian to go to space, tells us about his incredible journey. The only Indian to go to space, Ashok Chakra recipient and Hero of the Soviet Union, Rakesh Sharma is the name that every Indian takes pride in. Here is an interview with him-

Question: It has been almost 38 years since you became the first Indian to travel in space on Soyuz T-11.

How does it feel to be the only Indian to achieve this feat?

Rakesh Sharma: This has been unfortunate for the scientific community. I think my flight was premature in the sense that our country's space programme was not mature enough at that time to launch a manned space program. So, there was a lack of continuity.

Question: Tell us how it happened—your journey from selection to boarding the Soyuz?

Rakesh Sharma: Well, the Indian Space Research Organization (ISRO) was busy with its satellite programme and expressed a lack of interest. So, Mrs. Indira Gandhi, who was the Prime Minister at that time, further asked the IAF what their opinion was on the proposal and I got lucky!

Question: What was the reaction of your parents when they came to know that their son was going to become India's first astronaut?

Rakesh Sharma: Mixed, I guess. Pride, naturally, on the one hand, and anxiety on the other, because I was going to be exposed to a lot of risks.

Question: How different was the experience of traveling in a rocket from flying a fighter plane?

Rakesh Sharma: Very different. Since the space environment cannot be replicated on Earth, the training was limited to procedures and exposure, so it was not experiential. Essentially, procedures were practiced and the body was trained to handle the expected rigors of space travel. The actual experience mostly came from 'learning on the job'.

Question: Share with us your experience of the space mission. What did you do during your stay in space?

Rakesh Sharma: Actually, I was in space for about 190 hours. My day was filled with activities like setting up experiments, performing them, documenting the results, setting up the next experiment, and so on. In the meantime, I took time out for meals and interviews with dignitaries.

Question: 'Rakesh Sharma landed on the moon'—Why do you think this myth came into existence?

Rakesh Sharma: The concept of space travel was relatively unknown in our country. My guess is that the person on the street who was brought up on the stories/ songs of 'Chanda Mama' was associated with only the Moon in space. Furthermore, we can 'see' the Moon, while space itself is a vast, dark, gravity-defying vacuum with nothing around it!

Question: What qualities would you attribute your success to?

Rakesh Sharma: Being in the right place at the right time, being physically and mentally fit, being a qualified test pilot, having an open mind to try something new, and being lucky to make it.

Question: How did your parents influence your personality and your career choice?

Rakesh Sharma: They supported my decision to join IAF. They did not force me to pursue a career of their choice, instilled in me the spirit of hard work, motivated me to strive to be the best and made me realize my potential.

Question: As a parent, what qualities did you want to instill in your children?

Rakesh Sharma: To identify their passion and then let them follow it, whatever it may be. Plus, hard work and ethical conduct and I encouraged them to be thoughtful, curious, empathetic, multifaceted individuals with diverse interests.

Question: Your son, Kapil Sharma, is a successful film director. Your thoughts on how he decided to pursue a career in films instead of space science?

Rakesh Sharma: He had the freedom to choose his career. His school respected his sensitivity to the environment and he realized the power of films to send messages across on subjects close to his heart. Similarly, my daughter trained as a musician, singer, songwriter and textile designer, and now, she is a behavioural science professional.

Question: A biopic based on your life is going to be released soon. How does it feel to know that a film is being made about your life? And what do you hope to see in the film about your life?

Rakesh Sharma: I can't talk much about it because it is at the working stage and I have signed a non-disclosure agreement. Broadly speaking, it will document my journey and the challenges my family faced along the way.

Question: You have been awarded 'Ashoka Chakra' and 'Hero of the Soviet Union'. How does it feel to receive the highest honours from two countries?

Rakesh Sharma: I feel humbled.

Question: What were your feelings while reciting those famous lines 'Sare Jahan Se Achcha Hindustan Hamara'—while describing how our country looked like from space?

Rakesh Sharma: I was stating a fact. Our country looks beautiful from space. And, being a patriotic Indian who is proud of our inclusive culture, I was also pointing out the fact that there is more to our country than just looks!

Question: A lot has changed since you went to space although some aspects remain the same. Please explain in detail.

Rakesh Sharma: Yes. The human body will need to be trained as before because the effect of zero gravity on it has remained unchanged. Training techniques may be somewhat different today. For example, I trained according to the yoga system. I am unaware of the current training methods being employed to train space crews.

Question: What was the process through which you were selected?

Rakesh Sharma: The shortlist was prepared after scrutinizing the pilots' annual confidential reports. The list was shortened after medical tests were done. Finally, the selection was made among the test pilots.

Question: What did you do during 18 months of basic training? Which parts were the most challenging?

Rakesh Sharma: Training essentially involved learning about the spacecraft and its systems, simulator work to brush up on procedures, crew coordination and a lot of physical training to prepare the human body to face the rigors of space flight.

Question: Can you tell us something about psychological training?

Rakesh Sharma: Psychological assessment was conducted during the selection phase. Experts observed crew compatibility by subjecting team members to group tests. It should be remembered that all crew members with a flight background require minimal re-orientation when approaching the risk element associated with space flight. Hours spent as a team in simulator sessions polish off errors along with crew compatibility.

Question: You spent eight days in space. What did you do there? What is the most memorable part of that trip?

Rakesh Sharma: We conducted scientific experiments in the field of earth resources, bio-medical and physical science. The supreme beauty of our planet and witnessing the sunrise and sunset were the most memorable parts.

Question: When the world has already sent enough astronauts to space, what is the importance of India's effort now?

Rakesh Sharma: The world has already discovered a lot. Much more remains to be discovered. Space is the final frontier and a lot of human activities are being planned in space. India wants to develop its potential to be an equal player and contribute towards that challenging future.

Question: The Soviets/Russians have a set tradition that cosmonauts follow before every trip. Please tell us something about it.

Rakesh Sharma: It is a bit ironic that state-of-the-art scientific activities have been unable to dispel some superstitions. The Russians feel that Gagarin's flight was successful and that its pattern should be followed by every space crew for success. It has become a tradition to watch the film 'White Sun of the Desert' in the evening before the launch, wherein astronauts are being launched from Baikonur. It was Gagarin's favourite film and he saw it on April 11, 1961, a day before his launch.

Question: What is your advice to the astronauts in India?

Rakesh Sharma: I wish them well as they would build their career doing pioneering work like setting up colonies on the Moon and later on Mars. I would advise them to work towards establishing a more inclusive society in those remote places, where cooperation rather than competition becomes the norm.

Question: Do you think India should start a manned space programme?

Rakesh Sharma: Yes. I'm afraid we are already years behind in this business. This fact cannot be wished for. At some point in time, we will be forced to make use of the benefits of space technology.

Question: Indian scientists are more interested in launching satellites than in manned space flights. Do you want them to reconsider their priorities?

Rakesh Sharma: Priorities should be allocated by the government as they have a complete picture of the needs of the country. If the manned space programme is given priority, I believe we can change that. But it's going to be very expensive—the infrastructure and so on.

Question: If India opts for a manned space programme, will you take over the responsibility of training Indian astronauts?

Rakesh Sharma: We have direct knowledge of what it is. I am sure that Ravish Malhotra and I can do it. We just have to adapt the technology to our circumstances.

Question: Which technology is better—Russian or American?

Rakesh Sharma: It is difficult to compare. The Soviet philosophy is to proceed step by step. When they come up with something, their next model is an improvement. The Western technique is about hop, step and jump.

Question: How do you propose to use your space experience in your job in Air Force?

Rakesh Sharma: We became part of it only because it was a time-bound programme. From the time the next stage was allowed to proceed with, only a certain amount of time was available. The Soviet Union wanted a test pilot for this. All their astronauts are test pilots—they are exposed to cutting-edge technology in aviation. We were better equipped than others to get into the groove quickly. The concept was fairly simple, except for the language. That's how we became part of it, not because we were going to be involved in the space programme for the rest of our lives after the flight. But if some decisions are being taken, the knowledge we have acquired can certainly be put to good use.

Question: Do you think space travel will soon be possible for the common man?

Rakesh Sharma: Yes, in 20 to 25 years from now. With the shuttle already in place, it is logical to assume that this will be the next step. Of course, there must be valid reasons to travel to space! The capability already exists. The colonization of space is not far away.

Question: Where will all this lead?

Rakesh Sharma: The search for nearby planets will continue. Man will be able to move forward only after exhausting all the resources on earth and then interplanetary travel can take place. Theoretically, there are planets with an atmosphere that could support life. So far there is no evidence that there is actually life on other planets. It is only a matter of time before we know it.

Question: You have said that it is not 'Twinkle-Twinkle Little Star' in space. Then what is it really like?

Rakesh Sharma: Stars appear as pinpoints of light. They don't twinkle when we see them from Earth because there is no atmospheric blanket.

Question: Were your comments and statements on television spontaneous or prepared?

Rakesh Sharma: They were natural. If they went well, it's probably because I wasn't working under any motivational pressure!

Question: How much distance did you cover in space?

Rakesh Sharma: I spent eight days in space and travelled at the rate of 8 km per second. It was up to 5,529,600 km!

Question: When you went into space, did you experience a space shock like other people experience?

Rakesh Sharma: Not really. The media has covered the subject of space travel so well that I had a pretty good idea of what it was going to be like. You get shocks when you are not prepared for something. From Yuri Gagarin's flight to the landing on the moon and the landing of the shuttle, I studied everything very closely. Also, we did very good simulation exercises.

Question: How did it feel to be in space for eight days so far away from your family?

Rakesh Sharma: There was work as usual in space, too. There was work to be done till the last minute. There was no time to get bored or think of anything else.

Question: Did you experience fear while in space? Did you ever feel that you could get lost in space for some reason or the other and would keep circling the earth forever?

Rakesh Sharma: Not really. After learning the system, you know that every system has a backup and there is a backup for the backup. We were sure that everything would be fine.

Question: Did you face any particular difficulty while doing your work in space?

Rakesh Sharma: Yes. The problem was with zero gravity. For example, if you are brushing your teeth, you will need to tape your toes together. To do anything, you have to hold onto something else. We used an electric shaver with a vacuum cleaner attached to it.

Question: Was it difficult not to smoke while in space?

Rakesh Sharma: You should not smoke while in space. Anyway, I rarely smoke.

Question: What advice would you give to young people who follow you everywhere for autographs?

Rakesh Sharma: They should run for computer science; they are here to stay.

Question: Are you satisfied with the way India has progressed in the race for space?

Rakesh Sharma: Well, India was never a part of the race for space. That is the reason why it has come so far. I believe that this is the better way to know about it.

We must do our job. So far, we have done all the right things. We are in a position of survival today.

Question: Some people say that India should cut its space budget. What do you say?

Rakesh Sharma: It all depends on what your intention is. If your intention is to explore the Indian way of solving problems in space technology, as we have done, it is fine then.

Question: What do you want India to achieve in space now?

Rakesh Sharma: I would like it to be a voice that shapes an inclusive policy for human beings. We are on the threshold of starting space exploration. We are going to inhabit the Moon first followed by Mars. I wish we didn't do it alone and our own as it would be resource intensive. I don't think that this is the best way to use our resources given our other needs and compulsions. We are respected in the space community and can carry our weight for future missions. I am proud that India's space programme has achieved so much in such a short span of time.

Question: Do you think India's space mission has become political?

Rakesh Sharma: I don't think so.

Question: Any memory that you can share with us of your space mission?

Rakesh Sharma: I feel sorry that I am the only Indian who went to space, and that too 38 years ago. No other Indian has gone since then. I feel lonely in this sense. I also feel bad that my other two travel companions are no more. Of course, it was a life-changing moment for me. Space travel has impacted me a lot.

Question: What motivated you to continue your work even though you knew that you were risking your life a lot?

Rakesh Sharma: It was the passion that propelled me forward. I believe that it is important to overcome all our fears to do justice to our profession.

Question: How did you handle the sudden fame and how did you feel after that period ended?

Rakesh Sharma: If you are not used to something, you don't remember it when it is over.

Question: People want to buy land on the moon?

Rakesh Sharma: It is unfortunate because I believe that people will destroy outer space the same way they have destroyed Earth.

❑

Indian Space Program

The Indian space programme began in 1962. The Indian space programme was conceptualized by Dr. Vikram Sarabhai, who is called the father of the Indian space programme. He is known as a scientist and a national hero. In its present form, the programme is headed by the Indian Space Research Organization (ISRO).

Modern space research in India dates back to the 1920s when scientist S. K. Mitra conducted a series of experiments in Calcutta for the sound of the ionosphere by application of ground-based radio methods. Later,

Indian scientists like C. V. Raman and Meghnad Saha contributed to applied scientific principles in space science although it was the period after 1945 when significant developments were made in coordinated space research in India.

After independence in 1947, Indian scientists and politicians became known for their use of rocket technology in the security sector and the potential for R&D. With India being demographically large, the Space Research Organization was established in India considering the primary potential for artificial satellites in the field of telecommunications.

After the launch of Sputnik in 1957, they realized the usefulness of artificial satellites. India's first Prime Minister Jawaharlal Nehru, who considered scientific development to be an important part of India's future, placed space research under the supervision of the Department of Atomic Energy in 1961. Homi Bhabha, the director of the Department of Atomic Energy, who is considered the father of the Indian nuclear programme, formed the Indian National Committee for Space Research (INCOSPAR) in 1962 with Dr. Sarabhai as its chairman.

Like every major space programme, except Japan and Europe, India did it for the purpose of enabling artificial satellites to launch rather than to enable its known military missile programme. With the establishment of the Indian space programme in 1962, it started launching research rockets, in which its proximity to the equator proved to be a boon. All of them were launched from the newly established Thumba Mediterranean Rocket Research Centre, which is located near Thiruvananthapuram in South Kerala.

The Indian Space Research Organization was formed in 1969 from the INCOSPAR programme under the Department of Atomic Energy, which was initially working under the Space Mission, and consequently, the Department of Space was established in June 1972.

US Sanctions

India's cooperation with the Soviet Union in the field of booster technology was strongly resisted by the US under the guise of a non-proliferation policy. In 1992, the Indian organization ISRO and the Soviet organization Glavkosmos were threatened with sanctions. As a result of these threats, the Soviet Union withdrew from this cooperation. The Soviet Union was ready to give the cryogenic liquid rocket engine to India but it was not ready to provide the technology related to its manufacture, which India wanted to buy from the Soviet Union.

The result of this non-cooperation was that India, despite facing US sanctions, developed indigenous technology better than the Soviet Union after two years of tireless research. Although Russian engines are still being used in ISRO they are being replaced in a phased manner with indigenous technology.

The objective of the Indian space programme is to achieve self-reliance in the use of space science and technology for national development.

The main areas are-

1. Various national applications like telecommunications, TV broadcasting, satellite communication for AIR.
2. Resource survey and management by remote sensing, environmental investigation and meteorological services.
3. Development of indigenous satellites and launch vehicles to fulfill the above objectives.

Indian Space Research Organization (ISRO)

The Indian space programme was established in the year 1962 when the Indian National Committee for Space Research was formed. With this, the Indian Space Research Organization was added in 1969 and the Space

Commission and Department of Space was added in 1972. The Indian Space Research Organization is responsible for planning, executing and managing space research activities and space application programmes.

Other Affiliate organisations

- Vikram Sarabhai Space Centre: This is the main centre for the development of the launch vehicle located in Thiruvananthapuram.
- ISRO Satellite Centre: It is responsible for designing, building, testing and managing satellites located in Bangalore.
- Space Applications Centre: This is ISRO's R&D centre located in Ahmedabad for designing, organizing and manufacturing instruments for practical applications of space technology.
- SHAR Centre: This is the main launch centre of ISRO located at Sriharikota in Andhra Pradesh.
- Liquid Propulsion Instruments: It is a pioneer in the development of liquid and cryogenic propulsion for launch rockets and satellites. Its facilities are located in Thiruvananthapuram, Bangalore and Mahendragiri (Tamil Nadu).

- Development, Education Communication Unit: This centre located in Ahmedabad is engaged in conceptualization, definition, planning and socio-economic evaluation of space applications programme.
- Major Control Facility: This location at Hassan, Karnataka is responsible for all post-launch operations of INSAT satellites.
- ISRO Inactive Instruments Unit: This unit, located at Thiruvananthapuram, develops passive instruments for both satellites and launch vehicles.
- Physics Research Laboratory: This laboratory located in Ahmedabad comes under the Department of Space.
- National Remote Sensing Agency: This centre in Hyderabad investigates the Earth's resources.
- National Mesosphere, Stratosphere, Troposphere Radar Facility: Scientists use this facility at Gandaki, Andhra Pradesh to conduct atmospheric research.
- ISRO Inertial Systems Unit: IISU at Thiruvananthapuram conducts research and development work in inertial sensors and systems and related satellite elements.
- Electro-Optics Systems Laboratory: It performs research and development in the area of electro-optics

sensors and cameras required for LEOS satellites and launch rockets at Bangalore.

INSAT system

In the 1980s, INSAT system ushered in a major revolution in the communication sector in India. In this, eleven satellites - INSAT-4CB, INSAT-4B, INSAT-4A, EDUSAT, INSAT-3E, GSAT-2, INSAT-3A, Kalpana-1, INSAT-3C, INSAT-3B and INSAT-2E - are currently in service. The system provides a total of 66 C-band transponders, 8 broad C-band transponders and 3 KU-band transponders. Being a multi-purpose satellite system, it provides services in the areas of telecommunications, television broadcasting, weather forecasting, disaster warning and rescue.

Indian Remote Sensing Satellite System

Today, India has the largest set of remote sensing satellites, which serve at both national and global levels. The data is available through the Indian Remote Sensing Satellites (IRS) in various spatial resolutions, starting from 360 metres and going up to a resolution of 5.8 metres. State-of-the-art cameras on the IRS spacecraft capture images of Earth in different spectral bands. There are now 10 satellites operating in this group –

OCEANSAT-2, RISAT-2, CARTOSAT-2A, IMS-1, CARTOSAT-2, CARTOSAT-1, RESOURCESAT-1, TES, OCEANSAT-1 AND IRS. The Indian Earth Observation System with these satellites and a series of themes planned in the coming years, such as Megha-Tropiques, SARAL and INSAT-3D, is expected to provide innovative products and services for use in a wide range of areas ranging from cartography to climate.

Images sent by the IRS spacecraft are used in many ways in India. The most important in this is the estimate of the area and yield of crops in agriculture. Also, these pictures are used for information about water reserves. Surveys and management of forests and wasteland identification are other such uses.

Launch Vehicles

After the successful test of the first indigenous launch vehicle SLV-3 in 1980, ISRO built the next generation Augmented Satellite Launch Vehicle (ASLV). Our launch vehicle programme took a major leap forward in October 1994 with the launch of the IRS-P2 vehicle by the Polar Satellite Launch Vehicle. On April 18, 2001, India successfully launched a static satellite launch vehicle. India has the capabilities of Polar Satellite Launch Vehicle (PSLV) and Geostationary Satellite

Launch Vehicle (GSLV). The four-stage PSLV can launch satellites weighing up to 1600 kg into 800 kg polar orbit. It can also launch a one-tonne payload from a geostationary transfer orbit. GSLV can launch 2,500 kg class satellites into a geostationary transfer orbit.

Progress in the year 2009-10: ISRO has launched Radar Imaging Satellite Reset-2 to meet the defense needs of the country. Similarly, ISRO has successfully launched OCEANSAT-2, a state-of-the-art satellite for ocean research, by PSLB-C-14.

India's record of launching 104 satellites in space

India's biggest success in space - ISRO created history by launching a record 104 satellites simultaneously. PSLV, a launch vehicle of the Indian Space Research Organization (ISRO), successfully launched a record 104 satellites in a single mission from the space centre at Sriharikota on February 15, 2017. These 104 satellites included three from India and 101 from other countries. India became the first country to create history by sending 104 satellites into space with a single rocket.

Challenges before the Space Programme

- India lacks advanced technologies for training astronauts and launch vehicles for human spaceflight.

- Launch Vehicle, Launch Crew Module, Space Capsule Re-entry Technology, Life Support System, Spacesuit etc. are in the process of development.
- There is a need to enhance the technical proficiency of the Satish Dhawan Space Centre at Sriharikota for human spaceflight.
- The two Indian launch vehicles, Polar Satellite Launch Vehicle and Geosynchronous Satellite Launch Vehicle deployed to launch satellites and modules into space, are not yet 'man-rated' (a term used to measure the safety and integrity of a zero-failure launch vehicle).

Possibilities of Economic Use of Space

- At present, many companies in the world have joined the commercial race for space. These companies have encouraged the world to think about the economic use of space. Currently, the size of the global space industry is $350 billion. It is expected to grow to $550 billion by 2025.
- Thus, space is developing as an important market. ISRO has made significant achievements in the field of space. However, India's space industry is around $7 billion, which is only 2 percent of the global market.

Broadband and DTH services account for about two-thirds of India's space industry.

- According to ISRO, India will set up its own space station in space by 2030. Along with this, the 'Gaganyaan' project has also been approved to send a three-member crew to space by the year 2022. These projects will increase the possibilities of economic utilization by India's space programme.

Role of the Private Sector

- The role of the private sector in space-related activities has been limited in India. Private sector services have been availed only for less important tasks. ISRO still performs important tasks such as manufacturing and assembling equipment and testing.

- It is worth noting that NASA, the world's largest space sector institute, has also been taking help from the private sector. At present, there are more than 20 start-ups related to the new space in India. The approach of these enterprises is different from the traditional vendor/supplier model. These start-ups are exploring business opportunities either by directly engaging with the business or by directly engaging with the consumer.

- The way various independent app makers were allowed to access the Android and Apple platforms directly, it revolutionized smartphone usage. Similarly, by giving place to the private sector in the field of space, the possibilities of this sector can be increased and it will also be beneficial from India's point of view.

Chandrayaan Mission-1

- August 15, 2003: Announcement of Chandrayaan programme by the then Prime Minister Late Atal Bihari Vajpayee.
- October 22, 2008: Chandrayaan-1 was launched from Satish Dhawan Space Centre in Sriharikota.
- November 8, 2008: Chandrayaan-1 entered the Moon's transfer trajectory.
- November 14, 2008: The surface probe device ejected from Chandrayaan-1 and crashed near the Moon's south pole. Test confirmed the presence of water molecules on the Moon's surface.
- August 28, 2009: End of Chandrayaan-1 program.

Chandrayaan Mission-2

Chandrayaan-2, India's second lunar exploration mission, was launched by the GSLV version 3 launch vehicle.

The mission consisted of a lunar orbiter, a rover and a lander built in India. All of them were developed by ISRO. Chandrayaan-2 was successfully launched on July 22, 2019, at 2:43 pm IST from the Sriharikota range. But the Chandrayaan-2 lander deviated from its intended path and ground control lost communication with the spacecraft. On September 8, 2019, ISRO reported that the Vikram lander was detected by the thermal image taken by the orbiter, but Chandrayaan-2 could not be contacted.

Mangalyaan: India's First Mars Mission

Mangalyaan (Mars Orbiter Mission) was launched on November 5, 2013, at 2:38 pm to orbit Mars. A satellite was successfully launched by Polar Satellite Launch Vehicle (PSLV) C-25 from Satish Dhawan Space Centre in Sriharikota, Andhra Pradesh. With this, India also joined the countries that have sent their vehicles to Mars.

India's historic Mars Orbiter Mission (MOM), i.e., Mangalyaan, is still functioning well almost 5 years after its launch and entering the Martian orbit on September 24, 2014, and it is sharing the mission's essential images with ISRO and NASA. At present, some improvements will be made to the orbit of Mangalyaan so that it can work for many years.

According to sources associated with ISRO, efforts will be made to increase the life of its battery by improving the orbit of Mangalyaan. This is also necessary so that Mangalyaan continues to get energy even during long eclipses. If the orbit is not improved, it may become inactive as the battery can get exhausted during a long eclipse.

By the way, till now two-thirds of the campaigns that were started to get information on Mars have been unsuccessful. But by reaching Mars on September 24, 2014, India became the first country in the world to succeed in its first attempt and the fourth country in the world after Soviet Russia, NASA and the European Space Agency to reach Mars. Apart from this, it is also the least expensive mission sent to Mars.

India also became the first country in Asia to do so because earlier China and Japan had failed in their Mars mission. The prestigious 'Time' magazine named Mangalyaan one of the best inventions of 2014.

❖ On November 7, 2013, the first attempt to raise the orbit of Mangalyaan was successful.

❖ On November 8, 2013, the second attempt to raise the orbit of Mangalyaan was successful.

- ❖ On 9 November 2013, another orbit of Mangalyaan was successfully raised.
- ❖ Fourth successful attempt to raise the orbit of Mangalyaan on November 11, 2013.
- ❖ On November 12, 2013, the fifth attempt to raise the orbit of Mangalyaan was successful.
- ❖ On November 16, 2013, Mangalyaan was last raised in orbit.
- ❖ On December 1, 2013, Mangalyaan successfully left Earth's orbit and headed towards Mars.
- ❖ On December 4, 2013, Mangalyaan went out of orbit of the 9.25 lakh km circle of the Earth.
- ❖ The first improvements were made to the spacecraft on December 11, 2013.
- ❖ On September 22, 2014, Mangalyaan reached its final stage. Mangalyaan entered the gravitational field of Mars.
- ❖ Mangalyaan brought a historic moment for India with its entry into the orbit of Mars on 24 September 2014. With this, India became the first country in the world to achieve success in the Mars mission in the first attempt.

What is Mangalyaan doing now?

Mangalyaan, sent to find out about the presence of methane gas on Mars, is earning even after retirement. Although it was expected to work for only six months the US space agency NASA is buying pictures sent by it even after four years. Through them, NASA may soon reach a conclusion about the presence of methane on Mars.

All five instruments on board the Mangalyaan belong to ISRO, which are directly connected to the main control room at Hassan. According to ISRO, Mangalyaan will continue to work for the next three-four years. For the past several years, efforts have been going on to find out whether there is life outside the Earth or not.

India Achieved This Success at the Lowest Cost

With the successful Mars mission, India achieved a significant position in the entire world. Not only that, India achieved this success at the lowest cost. Approximately Rs 450 crores were spent on this entire campaign whereas a space-based film called 'Gravity' made in America had spent more money than this on its making. America spent 10 times more money than India on the Mars mission. After America, Russia and Japan, India became the fourth country to succeed in the Mars mission.

In the Mars mission, India achieved success on the very first attempt. This journey of 67 crore kilometres was not easy at all. Many experts worked hard in making this journey successful. Earlier, China's first Mars mission, Yanzhou-1, failed in 2011. Japan's first Mars mission in 1998 was unsuccessful as it ran out of fuel. From the year 1960 till now, 51 missions have been sent to Mars from around the world and their success rate has been 24 percent. Therefore, there was more pressure on the Indian campaign.

❑

Rakesh Sharma and Space Quiz

Who is Rakesh Sharma?

Answer: India's first astronaut.

When and where was Rakesh Sharma born?

Answer: January 13, 1949, in the city of Patiala, Punjab.

When did Rakesh Sharma go to space?

Answer: On April 3, 1984.

What was the name of Rakesh Sharma's space station?

Answer: Soviet Space Station, from where he left for space.

How many years of rigorous physical, mental and emotional training did Rakesh Sharma undergo along with his colleagues?

Answer: Two years.

Who were Rakesh Sharma's companions during the space journey?

Answer: Yuri Vasilyevich Malyshev and flight engineer Gennady Mikhailovich Strekalov.

How did Rakesh Sharma become an astronaut from a pilot?

Answer: Rakesh Sharma became Squadron Leader while working in the Air Force. Then he was sent to Baikonur in Kazakhstan, Soviet Union for training in the year 1982. After two years of rigorous physical, mental and emotional training, he became an astronaut from a pilot.

Who is the world's 138th astronaut?

Answer: Rakesh Sharma

When was Rakesh Sharma conferred the gallantry award 'Ashok Chakra'?

Answer: In 1985.

How old was Rakesh Sharma when he joined the Air Force in 1970?

Answer: 21 Years

With which award was Rakesh Sharma honoured by Russia?

Answer: 'Hero of the Soviet Union'.

During Rakesh Sharma's space flight, when Indira Gandhi asked him what India looked like, what was Rakesh Sharma's reply?

Answer: 'Sare Jahan Se Achcha Hindustan Hamara'.

Why was Rakesh Sharma honoured with 'Ashok Chakra'?

Answer: Rakesh Sharma was awarded 'Ashok Chakra' by the Government of India after successfully completing the space mission.

Which service opportunity did Rakesh Sharma get after retirement from the Indian Air Force?

Answer: Opportunity to serve as 'Test Pilot' in 'Hindustan Aeronautics Limited'.

Space: Other Important Q&A

Which is the first country to land a man on the lunar surface?

Answer: America.

What is the name of the first robotic spacecraft sent to explore the planet Venus?

Answer: Magellan.

Indian Space Research Organization was formed in 1969. Where are its headquarters?

Answer: Bangalore.

Who is the first Asian to go to space?

Answer: Pham Tuan (Vietnam, 1980).

Who was the first person to go into space?

Answer: Yuri Gagarin (Russia).

What is the new name of Sriharikota Space Centre located in Sriharikota in Andhra Pradesh?

Answer: Satish Dhawan Space Centre.

Who is the first woman to go into space?

Answer: Valentina Tereshkova (Russia).

Where was India's first remote sensing satellite launched?

Answer: Baikonur.

How much is the surface temperature of the Sun estimated to be?

Answer: 6000-degree centigrade.

Which is the first spacecraft to travel to the Moon?

Answer: Apollo-8.

Who is the first person to travel in space seven times?

Answer: Jerry Ross (USA, 2002).

How many constellations are there in space?

Answer: 89.

When was the Space Commission established by the Government of India?

Answer: 1972.

Under whom does the Indian Space Research Organization function as its research and development organization?

Answer: Department of Space.

What does the rising of the evening star represent?

Answer: East direction.

What method do we use in determining the age of the Earth?

Answer: Uranium dating.

First space animal?

Answer: A female dog named Laika.

Who first propounded that the earth rotates on its axis?

Answer: Copernicus.

When was the Indian Space Research Committee constituted?

Answer: 1962.

Which planet has the most satellites?

Answer: Jupiter

Which planet in the solar system is the most intense?

Answer: Mercury.

Where is the headquarters of the Space Commission?

Answer: Bangalore.

Who was the first person to swim in space?

Answer: Alexei Leonov (Russia, 1965).

Who is the first woman to spend the longest time in space, walk and participate in a marathon during her stay in space?

Answer: Sunita Williams (American citizen of Indian origin).

What is the region of extreme gravity at the centre of our galaxy which pulls all the matter in its region towards itself called?

Answer: Black hole.

Who is the first American woman to go into space?

Answer: Sally Ride (in 1983).

On which date the first indigenously built satellite INSAT-2A was launched into space?

Answer: On July 10, 1992.

What is the objective of the Indian Space Research Organization (ISRO)?

Answer: To plan, organize and implement the nation's growing activities in space science, space technology, and space applications.

Which is the first animal to go into space by rocket?

Answer: A monkey named Albert.

Name of America's first space shuttle?

Answer: Colombia.

Who is the first Indian-origin woman to go into space?

Answer: Kalpana Chawla.

Which planets lie between Mars and Uranus?

Answer: Jupiter and Saturn.

From where was India's first satellite launched?

Answer: From Russia's Cosmodrome.

With the space travel of Rakesh Sharma, India became ___ nation to send a man to space.

Answer: 14th.

The world's first space tourist?

Answer: Dennis Tito.

Who propounded the law of motion of the planets?

Answer: Kepler.

Which is the first weather satellite of India?

Answer: MATSAT (Kalpana-1).

When was the first satellite Aryabhata launched?

Answer: On April 19, 1975.

Name of the first unmanned buggy, which has the distinction of walking on the lunar surface.

Answer: Lunokhod-1 (Russia).

What is the full name of ISRO?

Answer: Indian Space Research Organisation.

The first female driver of the US Space Shuttle?

Answer: Eileen Collins.

In how many days does the planet Mercury complete one revolution around the Sun?

Answer: In 88 days.

Where was India's first communication satellite centre established?

Answer: In Arvi, Maharashtra.

Which was the first satellite of INSAT series?

Answer: INSAT-1.

Where is the cryogenic engine used?

Answer: In the space shuttle.

What is the number of countries in the world having satellite launch capability?

Answer: 7.

Which planet is called the 'God of Beauty'?

Answer: Venus.

Which was the first communication satellite of India?

Answer: Apple.

India's first woman space scientist?

Answer: Savita Rani.

When was the first Indian satellite 'Aryabhata' launched into space?

Answer: On April 19, 1975.

Who is credited with the beginning of space research in India?

Answer: Vikram Sarabhai.

On which date was India's first spacecraft Chandrayaan-1 successfully launched on the lunar surface?

Answer: October 22, 2008.

Name of the first commercial communication satellite?

Answer: Ali Bird.

Oldest astronaut?

Answer: Karl G. Henize.

Youngest astronaut?

Answer: Gherman Titov.

The first teacher to go into space?

Answer: Sharon Christa McAuliffe—USA.

First astronaut to go to space twice?

Answer: Colonel Vladimir Komarov.

The first person to exit the spacecraft.

Answer: Alexei Leonov - USA.

❑

References

In addition to various sources of information and personal contacts for writing the book, help has been taken from the following sources of information, for which the author has heartfelt gratitude.

'A rehabilitation tool for functional balance using altered gravity and virtual reality'. Journal of Neuroengineering and Rehabilitation.

- economictimes.indiatimes.com
- everageedu.com
- https://appearnews.com/know
- https://bansalnews.com/theAstoryg
- https://jiwanparichay.in/rakeshAsharmaAbiography AinAhindi/
- https://jiwanparichay.in/rakeshAsharmaAbiography AinAhindi/

- https://steemit.com/life/@mgibson/an
- https://vigyanprasar.gov.in/isw/IndiasAfirstAastronautArakeshAsharmaAhindi.html
- https://www.amarujala.com › Photo Gallery Bizarre News
- https://www.gnttv.com/science/story/happyAbirthday
- https://www.jagran.com/blogs/others/rakeshAsharma
- https://www.jionewstv.com/2021/02/BiographyAofAAstronautARakeshASharmaAinAHindi.html
- https://www.navodayatimes.in/news/khabre/rakeshAsharmaAtheAfirstAindianAastronaut/134439/
- https://www.parentcircle.com/interviewAwithArakeshAsharmaAfirstAindianAonAmoon/article
- https://www.samanyagyan.com/hindi/biography ArakeshAsharma
- https://www.theweek.in/theweek/cover/2018/09/21/rakesh
- https://www.timesnownews.com/theAbuzz/article/rakesh

- timesofindia.indiatimes.com
- www.aryaanstudycirclehs.com
- www.bbc.com
- www.bharatArakshak.com
- www.bhaskar.com
- www.freepressjournal.in
- www.indiaonline.in
- www.indiatoday.in
- www.latestgkgs.com
- www.newindianexpress.com
- www.timesnownews.com
- Astronaut training. Aviation Week and Space Technology. Morring F.
- Space Vehicle Mock-up Facility (SVMF). NASA.
- Virtual Reality-Based Space Operations— A study of ESA's potential for VR-based training and simulation.
- Virtual, augmented and mixed reality: Interaction, Navigation, Visualization. Springer International Publishing.
- Indian Journal of Physiotherapy and Occupational Therapy.

- Aerospace Medicine and Human Performance. A. B. C. Anderson, Allison P.
- Autonomic Neuroscience: Basic and Clinical.
- Can virtual reality help keep astronauts calm? Discover Magazine.
- Crew Training Safety: An Integrated Process, Safety Design for Space Systems, Burlington: Butterworth-Heineman.
- Selection and Training, Space Security and Human Performance, Butterworth-Heineman.
- Preparing for the Launch: Astronaut Training Process. A.B.C. Seedhouse, Eric.
- Aviation, Space and Environmental Medicine. AB Stroud, Kenneth J.; Harm, Deborah L.; Kloss, David M.
- Space Motion Sickness. Autonomic Neuroscience: Basic and Clinical.
- Heavy Ion Carcinogenesis and Human Space Exploration. Durante, M. and F. A. Cucinotta.